P9-CCD-476

TIGER TROUBLE!

DIANE GOODE

SCHOLASTIC INC.

New York   Toronto   London   Auckland   Sydney
Mexico City   New Delhi   Hong Kong   Buenos Aires

FOR PETER

No part of this publication may be reproduced in whole or in part,
or stored in a retrieval system, or transmitted in any form or by any means,
electronic, mechanical, photocopying, recording, or otherwise, without
written permission of the publisher. For information regarding permission,
write to Scholastic Inc., Attention: Permissions Department,
555 Broadway, New York, NY 10012

This book was originally published in hardcover by the Blue Sky Press in 2001.

ISBN 0-439-20867-X

Copyright © 2001 by Diane Goode
All rights reserved. Published by Scholastic Inc.
SCHOLASTIC and associated logos are trademarks and/or
registered trademarks of Scholastic Inc.

12 11 10 9 8 7 6 5 4 3 2 1   2 3 4 5 6 7/0

Printed in the U.S.A.   24

First Scholastic paperback printing, January 2002

Designed by Kathleen Westray

JACK AND HIS TIGER, LILY,

lived in an apartment building

at #33 River Street.

Everything that Jack did,

Lily did.

And everything that Lily did,

Jack did.

Everywhere that Lily went,

Jack went.

And everywhere that Jack went,

Lily followed.

They did not have a care

in the world.

Until . . .

. . . the terrible, horrible day when Mr. Mud bought

the apartment building at #33 River Street . . .

. . . and moved in upstairs with his dog, Fifi.

Mr. Mud did not like cats

of any kind.

And neither did Fifi.

So, when Mr. Mud and Fifi met Lily,

it was a shock!

"That cat could scare someone!" cried Mr. Mud.

"I want her gone by tomorrow morning!"

"Lily scare someone? Never!

We will find a way for you to stay!" cried Jack.

They thought and thought, but they could not
think of a way to keep Lily.

Finally, they went to bed.

But Lily could not sleep.

Outside she heard a noise.

Looking out the window, she saw a burglar

climbing into Mr. Mud's apartment . . .

. . . where he began to fill a sack

with all of Mr. Mud's favorite things . . .

. . . including Fifi.

Just as he was making his escape,

Lily came running to the rescue.

The burglar's screams woke up Mr. Mud . . .

. . . who rushed in, just in time

to see Lily save poor Fifi.

Now everyone in the building was awake.

Lily stood guard over the burglar,

while Mr. Mud called for the police.

The police arrested the burglar.

Everyone cheered,

"HOORAY FOR LILY!"

By morning, everyone knew

that Lily was a hero . . .

. . . and Mr. Mud begged Lily not to go.

So did Fifi.